# Becka and the Big Bubble
## Becka Goes to India

by Gretchen Schomer Wendel and
Adam Anthony Schomer

Illustrated by Damon Renthrope

*for Brent, Benjamin, and Dave*

Published in 2009 by Windmill Books, LLC
303 Park Avenue South, Suite # 1280, New York, NY 10010-3657

Publisher Cataloging Data
Wendel, Gretchen Schomer
     Becka goes to India / by Gretchen Schomer Wendel and Adam Anthony Schomer ;
illustrated by Damon Renthrope.
          p. cm. – (Becka and the big bubble)
     Summary: Becka blows her way to India, where she makes new friends who take her to the
Taj Mahal, a Hindu wedding, and more.
     ISBN 978-1-60754-110-3 – ISBN 978-1-60754-111-0 (pbk.)
ISBN 978-1-60754-112-7 (6-pack)
     1. India—Juvenile fiction    2. Travel—Juvenile fiction   [1. India—Fiction  2. Travel—Fiction
3. Bubbles—Fiction   4. Stories in rhyme]   I. Schomer, Adam Anthony   II. Renthrope, Damon
III. Title   IV. Series
     [E]—dc22

Printed in the United States of America

alphabet
soup™

an imprint of

WINDMILL
BOOKS
New York

Becka closed her eyes

And imagined what to do.

She blew and blew and **blew** and **blew**...

Flippity-Free!

This time she blew a double!

## To far away INDIA
## Flew Becka and the Big Bubble!

Past the Himalayas,
Such skill to fly through
And vast grassy plains.
The wind how it blew.

There was even an ocean by India's own name
And wondrous elephants decorated in fame.

Mumbai* is full of people

As far as one can see.

"Nobody here

Looks quite like me!"


"What's that they're burning?

Crazy cool smell."

That incense is hot

**POP** and she fell.

*Mumbai (mum-bī), formerly known
as Bombay, is India's largest city.

Gliding through the air
Becka now fell

Caught by new friends—
Their secrets they'd tell.

She rode on an elephant, as a welcomed new friend.

She saw in their smiles, this was not pretend.

To the Taj Mahal, a place built out of love,

Smoothly carved marble, as white as a dove.

Onto Jaipur*, the lovely pink city,

Hand crafted pots and carpets so pretty.


Up on the rooftops, kids flying kites,

Dotting the skies, what a wonderful sight.


*Jaipur (jī-pôr) is known for its celebration of India's kite festival.

After the kite festival
It was time to eat.
"Yippidi-Dee!
This looks so neat!"

Inside of the home,
A feast to come soon,
Yet she saw no chairs,
Not even a spoon.

This culture is different, some eat with their hands.

And then Becka thought…"THIS IS MY KIND OF LAND!"

She dipped bread in dips, dips they call Dahl,

Each ever more spicy, Becka tried them all.

Next a Hindu wedding, bride and groom seated,
Showered with gifts, as their guests came and greeted.

Laughing and loving, for days this can last.
"A three day party, that sounds like a blast!"

That bald man is noble.

"Who's he?" Becka asked.

"Gandhi," they said,

Their smiles so vast.


He fought for the people.

He fought without fists.

He's one fine fellow

The world does miss.


And as if to answer,

The music began

From behind the wall.

To hear, Becka ran.

Beats from the Tabla, a wet sounding drum.
The Sitar is relaxing like a sweet guitar's hum.

Both of these sounds are native to this land.
Becka closed her eyes to feel the band.

Then all of her friends danced in delight.
Becka now felt how music takes flight!

Together they **blew music bubbles** in tune.
Becka floated off toward the glorious moon.

"Good-bye India, a beautiful land!
I hope to come back to a country so grand."

And before she knew it she could see Mom and Dad.
"Pop on in, time for supper I'm glad."

**Pippity-Pop!**

With the flick of her nail

To the ground she sailed...

What a day it had been!

Gretchen Schomer Wendel graduated from Michigan State University. After college she worked as a television reporter and writer on an award winning show in San Francisco. She has now written numerous children's books. Gretchen spends most of her spare time with her two children and her husband. They reside in San Diego, California.

Adam Schomer is a writer, actor, and improv comedian who was an All Ivy Athlete at Cornell University. Through soccer he explored the world, and it gives him great joy to share his traveling experience and life lessons through Becka. Adam continues to also write plays, sketch comedy, and animated TV.

Damon Renthrope is an award-winning illustrator in San Diego, California. After attending San Diego State University, he's created art for Rohan Marley, Mandy Moore, and various companies including DC Shoes, Sideout, Nascar, and MTV. He is most noted for his collection of caricature art, which features stylized portraits of famous faces. Selected works can be found on DamonArts.com.

You can go to www.windmillbks.com and select this book's title to find links to learn more about Becka and her adventures, or to watch and listen to Becka online.